Where's my daddy?

Adapted from a Story by
Shigeo Watanabe
Pictures by Yasuo Ohtomo

PERSEVERANCE

PHILOMEL BOOKS

Where's my daddy?
I can find him all by myself.
Maybe he's under
these dandelions.

No!

Oh, hello, birds.
Have you seen my daddy?

Hello, Cat.
Have you seen my daddy?

Sorry!
I have no time to talk!

Hello, Milkman.
Have you seen my daddy?

No!

Hello, Paper Seller.
Have you seen my daddy?

No, but I left his newspaper
at your house.

Hello, Letter Carrier.
Have you seen my daddy?

No! But I have a letter for him.

Hello, Mommy.
Have you seen Daddy?

No,
but I've got a kiss for you.

Thank you, Mommy,
but I'm still looking for Daddy.

Hello, Daddy! There you are!

I found you
all by myself!

E   C.2
Watanabe, Shigeo, 1928-
    Where's my daddy?
                            8.95

	DATE DUE		
APR 1 5 1998			